I'll Have a Glass of Water While I'm Waiting

D B Waite

DEDICATION

For my wonderful husband who put this book together and is the inspiration for some of the work in it.

(It's a shame he doesn't realise it!)

Thanks also go to my young friend Ella for her clever illustrations.

CONTENTS

READY WHEN YOU AREN'T

I'll have a glass of water while I'm waiting,
Although the time is nearly half past four
Since ten to two, my husband's been relating
How, without his phone, he won't walk through the door.
I'll have some tea and biscuits while I'm waiting,
By now it's almost twenty-five past five,
He cannot find his wallet, how frustrating
So I'm leaning on the car, still in the drive.
I'll have a large Prosecco while I'm waiting,
As his Sat Nav, now, is nowhere to be found
I've never met a man so aggravating,
And his capacity for losing things astound.
I'll have a four-course dinner while I'm waiting,
We should have left home several hours ago,
Does he need to use the loo, he's contemplating?
Yes, he does, but says he'll only be a mo.
I'll have some mints and coffee while I'm waiting,
I've given up all thoughts of going out
The whereabouts of car keys we're debating
And I'm amazed that I have curbed the urge to shout.
I'll have a cup of cocoa while I'm waiting,
As the Fire Brigade are on their way to me,
After twenty years of Hugh's procrastinating
I've locked him in the shed, and 'lost' the key.

DON'T THROW THAT AWAY – IT MIGHT COME IN HANDY

My husband has a shed, into which would fit a bed
If it wasn't for the stuff already there,
He's got mowers, forks and spades, in a variety of shades
But there isn't space for him to put a chair.
There are several broken trugs, outdated pellets for the slugs
And jars of food to help the flowers bloom,
Junk is piled up to the roof, if you needed any proof
That he doesn't have a single inch of room.
Leaky hoses, bits of string that can't be used for anything,
And an aerator to keep the lawns alive,
I don't know why it has been kept, as I remember how he wept
When the handle broke, in 1985.
There's a barrow with a puncture, whose use escapes me, at this juncture,
But I'm sure there'll be a cunning plan for that,
And lurking in the corner, like a sinister Jack Horner
Is a spider 'bout the size of next door's cat.

There are tools he's never needed, and advice he hasn't heeded
And a pile of God-knows-what stacked on the floor,
Beneath a heap of sacks and rags reside a couple of 'old lags'
And I found Lord Lucan crouched behind the door.
There's a gnome without a head somewhere inside the garden shed,
That I'm sure will come in handy, given time,
Tins of paint that lack their lids, a wooden sledge without its skids
To give away such 'treasures' is a crime.
Now he wants to have a bar, which is going much too far

Though my opinion was dismissed with just a shrug,
As I made it very clear, drinking vodka, gin and beer
Was hardly going to get the garden dug.
He has such a lack of space, I was informed, with a straight face,
That he needs another shed for "overflow",
He can't throw anything away that he might utilise one day
So a second shed's the answer, don't you know?
But I made a sound suggestion counteracting his congestion
What our US cousins like to call "curve ball",
If he really can't decide what to keep or cast aside
Then I'll "request" he just disposes of it all.

SMARTY PANTS

My husband bought a Smart Meter, quite unbeknownst to me
So he could monitor my use of electricity.
He nips out to the laundry room and waits around, nay lurking
So he can check the charge and which appliances are working.
He stands in front quite mesmerised and doesn't make a sound
As he watches units adding up and whizzing round and round.
Now, at this point I must explain the way our household works
As my husband feels entitled to several manly perks,
Like when I do the washing, any underwear that's mine
If weather's good, is hung outside and dried upon the line,
But I cannot do the same with his, so have to play it safe
As he says his pants go hard and stiff and ultimately chafe.
I must confess it makes no sense in any way to me
To use a tumble dryer when the sun and wind are free.
But, in he comes complaining that the meter's going mad
And every single second, that's another pound to add,
So why is the dryer running to accumulate such cost?
This I've been anticipating and preparing my riposte
So I'll just sit there quietly, while he winds down from his rants
And tell him what's inside are his pyjamas, socks and pants.

TALK TO ME

Can anyone explain to me the mania for Texting?
As it really is a mystery to me
And what about its saucy cousin, better known as
'Sexting'?
Is that a case of what you get, you see?

I gather 'sexting's' raunchy notes you write when all alone
Sent with naughty bits in photos, snapped 'al fresco'
I hope they use the camera on a private mobile phone
And don't utilise the photo booth in Tesco.

When I was young, we had a very much more simple life
With mates we used to meet up with, and talk to
But now that bloody texting's taken over and is rife
We text our friends in houses we can walk to.

We'll send a text to all of them suggesting that we meet
Ask by text whose turn it is to buy the round
And text about the menu saying what we'd like to eat
So we'll talk with no one uttering a sound.

We check our texts in restaurants and we check on them in
bars
And we're reading any updates while we jog
We ignore that it's illegal, so we're texting from our cars
And some even text while perching on the bog.

So just stop with the texting, as it's very rude you see
And it's a habit causing mayhem to the nation
There is no need to text when you are sitting next to me
Now switch off that phone, let's have a conversation.

MEDIUM RARE

I once went to a séance, as I'm curious to know
What happens when you pass away, is there somewhere to go?
Do the good folks head to Heaven while the bad ones go to Hell?
I thought at a mystic session, there'd be someone who could tell.
We sat round in a circle, holding hands, the way you do
And hoped the dear departed would be waiting to "come through".
Madame Blanc-Mange informed us to await her Spirit Guide
And then she turned off all the lights, what do they have to hide?
She told us "He's an Indian Chief, whose name is Dancing Bear
And he looks very handsome with his feathers in his hair".
We gathered he's a Shaman who came from the Great Plains
Well, that's a lot more interesting than Adrian from Staines.
With her Spirit Guide upon her, Madame went into a trance
Said our unearthly relatives were waiting for the chance
To have contact with their loved ones, so she called out several names
As she had messages to give, at least, that's what she claims.
She never asked for Egbert, Theodore or Bernadette
But Susan, Ann and Mary were the best that she could get.
The thing that really made me doubt, and I still don't understand
Was she asked "Is anybody there?" as if it wasn't planned:
"Knock once for yes and twice for no". I really can't help mocking
For if the spirit isn't here, then who the hell is knocking?

6

MRS MALAPROP DIAGNOSES

I fink I've got a touch of Arfer Wrightus in me fumb
An' I'm fairly sure that Asteroids are forming up me bum.
'ad Aviation Flu a time or two, Brucey Dozes from me 'ogs
An' I caught that blasted Pervy Virus from me neighbour's dogs.
Recently I 'ad a dose of Sticky Coaties caused by parrots
An' I've got Erotomeania from overeating carrots.
Me dentist tells me there is Ginger Lighters in me gums
If I don't brush 'em prop'ly, I'll 'ave dentures, like 'is mum's.
There's Decathletes 'oof Inflection growing in between me toes
An' an outbreak of Rhino-itis causing trouble up me nose.
But the very worst I've ever 'ad an' one with constant tingles
Is Most Pathetical Nostalgia that's left over from me Pringles.

7

I DON'T BELIEVE IT......

"Free to good home:
Cats with nine lives.
Only one remaining".

"Firm of Solicitors require secretary.
Shorthand and typing essential.
Must be discreet and prepared to take anything down."

A Wedding Anniversary Question You Shouldn't Ask:
"Do you still love me now that I'm fat, bald and have hairy ears?
Of course I do, darling.
You're my wife".

Sparks Electricians.
"The quality of our work will shock you".

"Marriage is like constipation.
Years of strain and nothing to show for it".

Lorst and Gorne Removals.
"We will gladly send your furniture to the four corners of the earth".

Tosser and Turner Beds.
"All you need for a good night's sleep.
Memory foam mattresses a speciality.
If we remember."

Ille, Gottern and Gaines, Financial Management.
"Invest with us and we'll show you what we can do with your money".

U'N'I.COM

I've never had much luck with men, because I'm rather shy
So thought I'd try the Internet, as time is passing by
I took the plunge with online dating, and goodness, what a choice
Even I could find a bloke on here, I'll have someone soon, rejoice.
So, filling in the questionnaire, do I want 'short or tall'?
As this is very new to me, I thought "I'll tick them all",
Professional or creative, sporty, wealthy, dark or fair?
I'm really not that bothered, as long as he's got teeth and hair. (His own, preferably)
Then I filled in all my details and they emailed me my matches
And the fellas they suggested, were all described as 'catches'.
I assumed their info was correct, the photographs were recent
And the Agency looked out for fibs, and snaps of parts indecent. (Silly me!)
I liked the look of one guy, a fireman, he said
But when I delved a little deeper, I'd been totally misled,
His picture was quite accurate, though his profile had a twist
He was not a proper fireman but convicted arsonist.
So, I carried on my searching, convinced I'd find another
But the photo wasn't him, it was his handsome, younger, brother.
He said he had a sense of humour, and I like a man who's funny

But he dressed like Lily Savage, and he didn't carry money.
Then I had a date for dinner with an architect named Hugh
Whose manners at the table were reminiscent of the zoo.
My next match was a dentist, a crashing bore called Ross,
His total conversation covered fifty ways to floss.
My last try with professionals, a solicitor named Dick
Intuitively christened, and terminally thick.
So, I tried 'creative', with a 'famous lookalike'
But he was not one I expected, so I told him "On your bike"
The picture that he posted made my senses go all swoony
But that's because the one he used was actually George Clooney.
Now wouldn't it be lovely if 'Gorgeous George' shared my boudoir?
But a Peter Pan impersonator's going much too far.
I was determined I would give it just one more, and final go
There has to be a man for me, somewhere, I just know.
So I picked a 'sporty' mountaineer. By now, I should know better
As he was fat and forty, and his mum had made his sweater.
He was wearing baggy purple shorts that came down to his calf
And the legend on his T-shirt proclaimed 'Love God'. No, don't laugh.
He had the most enormous tat, a green and purple rose
Which, strangely, was in keeping with the bolt stuck through his nose.

My 'Mountaineer' had never even scaled the smallest
hillock
And I have to tell you, frankly, that he looked a proper
pillock.
I've given up my membership, thus saved myself a wedge
And I've moved in, with the young man, who came round
to trim my hedge.

(No, that is not a euphemism!)

STALEMATE

When Mr Always Wright married Mrs Never Wrong
Their wedded bliss did not remain harmonious for long;
For Mr Always Wright was cross she wouldn't take his name
Even though traditionally they're usually the same.
But there was much hilarity when she explained her plight
As Mrs Never Wrong… was now Mrs Never Wright.
But wait! We have diversity, equality and things
With added complications that such freedom often brings
So Mr Always Wright should prove he's totally "on song",
And without delay must change his name to Mr Always Wrong..

OVERSTOCKED

My wife has several wardrobes, which are full up to the
brim
With clothes and shoes and handbags that she's
purchased on a whim,
But she's not a shopaholic, as she'll tell me in a flash
Since she's always very careful when parting with my
cash.
She "considers each investment", I felt myself turn pale,
And everything she's got, she says, she picked up in a
sale.
Who can resist a bargain when some items are a prize?
Does it really matter if the shoes are the wrong size?
The fact that they are half the price is all that really counts
So like a cat upon a mouse, instinctively, she'll pounce.
There are coats too big, tops too small, and suits she'll
never wear
And hats that are quite awful, but she really doesn't care
She won't get rid of anything that she might wear 'one day'
So I'll have a massive clear-out and I'll give it all away.
That's what I did, and have to say that in my own defence
I don't think I'll be convicted – as it is my first offence.

*(Author's Note: My husband said that as I had written a verse about
men and their sheds, I should do one for women and their wardrobes).*

FUNNY YOU SHOULD ASK...........PART 1

If a clergyman is suspected of committing a crime, is he a parson of interest?

Could a crustacean starring in an adult movie, be considered a prawn star?

Is a crook who is clever with words, a lexicon?

Would you say an overweight monk with a fascination for philosophy, is a deep, fat, friar?

Has an accountant who absconds with his neighbour's cat, run off with the kitty?

Is a bus full of elderly shoemakers, a load of old cobblers?

If an NCO disciplines his child, is that corporal punishment?

Would you say a person deliberately committing an offence in a marquee, is guilty of criminal intent?

Should you criticise your host's choice of wine, would it be considered a remark in questionable taste?

If a bricklayer leaves his job, has he thrown in the trowel?

HEAT EXCHANGE

"The boiler needs replacing", my husband said to me
"It's getting far too old to work at all efficiently,
I'll look around and find us one that's elegant and sleek
And one that won't have breakdowns, several times a week."
Now our old boiler served us well for nigh on forty years,
At the thought of a replacement, I shed bucket-loads of tears.
It has been a faithful servant all through times both thick and thin,
But now my mate's decided that it's time to trade it in.

In recent months I've noticed that it hasn't been the same,
The pilot light has turned into a slowly dimming flame.
It needs a little notice now to get the water 'warm',
And tepid baths and showers are very much the norm.
It used to work in silence, you'd not know that it was there,
We had so much hot water, that we had enough to spare.
But when it fires up these days, it whistles and it moans,
Then the central heating pipes join in with creakings and with groans.

It takes about a week now, for the pipes to all get hot,
And suddenly they make a noise like someone fired a shot.
Just when everything has settled down, they do it once again,
Sending gallons of hot water, wasted, gushing down the drain.
I'll be sad to see the boiler leave when it goes out the door,
As it was a new appliance back in nineteen sixty-four.
We've shared a lot between us, but it's time to say "goodbye",
Before it throws a wobbler and shoots us up into the sky.
My man's in seventh heaven, the new heater is installed,
When home from work that evening, to his study I was called,
And sitting in there with him, was a girl of twenty-three,
The old boiler he's replacing, is, obviously me.

OH, MY GODFATHERS!

My passport needs renewing, so I had my photo done
But why is it they never seem to flatter anyone?
I refrained from smiling, and I didn't wear a scowl
Though when I saw my picture, my instinct was to howl.
So if ever there's a vacancy, I'm sure I'd get the job
As the image makes me look like an enforcer for The Mob.

WELSH RAREBIT

My sis and I were looking
For a brand-new three-piece suite
Before we drove to the Emporium
We thought that we would eat.
So we dressed up very smartly,
Like ladies do, who do lunch
And found a local 'Gastropub'
To sit, and chat, and munch.
When we had finished eating
We went into the store
And the friendly male assistant
Told my sis "We've met before
I'm sure I've seen you somewhere
Do you come from Wales?
I'm convinced I've seen you walking………."
Stony silence then prevails.
He dug himself in deeper
Said "I think I know the place
It's on the streets of Tenby
I don't forget a face".
I was absolutely horrified
Thought I'd not heard him right,
That he'd insinuate my sister
Was a lady of the night.
Another thing annoyed me:
She was wearing my best jacket,
Just as well he stepped away
Before I punched him up the bracket.

NO, YOU'RE NOT

I'm, like, writing you this rhyme
It's how I like to spend my time
And, like, I really hope you'll see which way I'm leaning
As I just don't like the way
The, like, youngsters of today
Use "like" but never understand the meaning.

I've, like, been spending several hours
As I like to, sniffing flowers
And, like, talking to my friends upon the phone
Just because I like to say
I don't, like, have the time today
Would you like to spend tomorrow on our own?

Is there, like, anything at all
Maybe someone you'd like to call
Or, like, shall we go somewhere and grab a coffee?
Perhaps you'd like to shop
But, like, tell me when to stop
Would you like a skinny latte topped with toffee?

Does, like, anybody function
Who likes the term 'conjunction'?
Or, is, like, 'preposition' more your kind of word?
Do you like to spend your day
In, like, an adjectival way?
But I don't like an adverb used when it's absurd.

WIND TUNNEL TESTED - NOT

There was a young man called Fred Smale
Who purchased a wig in a sale,
When he let out a sneeze
It blew off, in the breeze,
Now he keeps it secured with a nail.

HEAVY LIFTING

My husband spoke some words I dread –
"I've booked a holiday" he said.
"With lots of lovely food and booze –
We're going on a four- week cruise".
He knows I hate to be away,
I don't know what to wear each day.
He only ever takes one case
For months of moving place to place,
Two shirts, three trousers, pants and socks
His suitcase shuts, and even locks.

He told me "This year, travel light"
Which guaranteed a sleepless night,
He doesn't mean to be unkind,
But, what do I take or leave behind?
I laid my clothes out, on the bed
"Put half away" my sister said,
I'm feeling stressed, I want to laugh
For how do I decide which half?
I might wear these, I might want those,
Dresses, trousers, tops in rows.
Four pairs of shorts will go with that –
Has anybody seen my hat?

My suitcases are by the door,
But now I'm thinking "Just one more,
I haven't packed my bags and shoes
How can we ladies ever choose?"
I need someone to tell me "Stop!
Just shut the case and sit on top".
My husband said "You've gone too far
There's no more room inside the car".
He's got my cases, eight in all
But left me standing in the hall.

OH, NO HE ISN'T

I am not a Panto person
As my wife will quite agree,
And if I never see another one
Then that's all right with me.
I do quite like 'The Theatre'
For intellectual stuff
But Panto is so juvenile
I've really had enough.
There are men dressed up as women
And the women dress as men
But when you think you've worked it out
They all change back again.
Widow Twankey's not a woman
And Aladdin's not a man,
But "he" always seems to get the girl
Explain that, if you can.
Now, take for instance 'Hamlet'
Or 'The Taming of the Shrew',
You don't shout "He's behind you"
Nor do you hiss and boo.
And they won't ask horrid children
To recite "Alas, poor Yorick"
While fondly doting parents
Sit there Tweeting, quite euphoric.
So, don't invite me to the Panto
As it's an offer I'll refuse,
But will meet you in the Interval
And drown myself in booze.

LOCATION, LOCATION

When men go shopping, why is it
A monumental task?
When most can't track down what they want
Why won't they go and ask?

And if their item's out of stock
They'll buy something else instead
My husband went in for a bulb
And came out with a shed.

A shop assistant passed him by
Her face a neutral mask
She knows where all the stock's displayed
But would my husband ask?

And when the Sat Nav got him lost
He claimed, "It's loose connections",
But what no man will ever do
Is stop, and ask directions.

FOREIGN TRAVEL

My husband, Seymour, loves me, and just to show he cares
He's invested in a Chair Lift, to get me up the stairs.
He doesn't want a Churchill and a Stannah holds no sway
So he's gone all continental, and he's bought a Trebuchet.

To be completely honest, it's rather left me all at sea
But he's certain it will solve the problems that he has with me.
He saw it on the telly in those re-enactment shows,
And because he just adores me, and what's best for me, he knows,
He found one on the internet, an ex-display, quite cheap
That might become an heirloom, therefore something he could keep.
It comes complete with boulders, though I'm not sure what they're for
And it's not fixed to the bannisters but stands upon the floor.
He wanted me to try it out the moment it arrived
So he put it all together, though it looked a bit contrived.
It only had the one control, a lever at the back
And several ropes and pulleys, to take up all the slack.
He heaved me in the bucket, by no means an easy feat
Which I must confess surprised me, I thought stair lifts had a seat.
He fiddled with the lever and I'm sure he said "goodbye"

Then I was catapulted up the stairs and on into the sky.
I left the loft in ruins as I hurtled into space
With a ton of rubble in my hair, and plaster on my face.
He didn't seem at all concerned but acted most aloof
And shouted "While you're passing, can you just check out the roof?
How many tiles are missing, does the chimney need repair?
'Cos I won't have to bother if you do it while you're there".

I called "hello" to the neighbours, who looked shocked as I flew past
And I landed thirty metres up, astride their TV mast.
They contacted the Fire Brigade, who kindly helped me down
They must think my husband's funny, as one said he was a clown.
The Trebuchet's on eBay now, but not had any bids
Nobody seems to want it, not to even scare their kids.
My Seymour, who still loves me, so much, that he's in tears
Denied, when asked, intended harm, but still got seven years!

SURELY NOT?

Some men won't throw anything away in case it comes in handy.
If it does, they can't find it.

If someone says "I'm speechless," how do they carry on talking?

I've stopped cooking with wine as it meant I had to share it.

If a man says he loves you with all his heart, it doesn't necessarily include his wallet.

My husband says I'm naturally argumentative.
No!
I'm not!!

Do male gynaecologists ever have a hard day at work?

You're my best friend, so I'd give you the shirt off my back.
But get away from that last glass of wine.

Generosity is a wonderful thing, especially if you can give away someone else's last penny.

Family history research has a lot of dead ends.

THE LOSER

My husband is a loser, although not the way you think
The only thing he's not misplaced is probably the sink.
Over many years we've hunted for items such as these
Pens and pencils, phones and hats, single gloves and
keys.
He has them to begin with, then they start to go astray
And I've often heard him saying "Well, I had them
yesterday
I know I've put them somewhere safe, I can't remember
where
But I've got a funny feeling that I left them over there".
I really wouldn't mind so much, the truth I have to tell
It's not just his stuff he can't find, but things of mine, as
well.
He'll pick things up and put them down, completely
unconcerned
I get quite cross as this occurs at times my back is turned.
And when I ask him where he's put my favourite kitchen
knife
He'd better hope it can't be found while anger is still rife.
It isn't only little things, I have to tell you that
In fact, it's now been several months since I last saw the
cat.
I'm sure he's put it somewhere and I wish he would
remember
I can't recall it's been around since some time in
December.
My husband wanders round the house in something of a
fog,
He asked me just the other day if I had seen the dog.
"We haven't got a dog" I said "Not had one for a spell"
His face lit up with joy because he'd not lost him as well.
I really think the answer is to tie his hands together
Or I'll dig a grave at midnight when we get some better
weather.

HAIR RAISING

When we had friends who came to stay
We thought we'd go out for the day,
As Stourhead is not too far
We headed off there, in the car.
After we parked and went inside
And there were welcomed by the Guide,
She handed each of us some maps
And what I thought were shower caps.
I assumed the ceiling's being painted
And my hair with drips might be acquainted,
So as I put them on my head

My friend nudged me and loudly said:
"You haven't got the first of clues –
You're supposed to put them on your shoes".

*(Author's Note: Said friend tells me I shouldn't be allowed out alone.
She may have a point).*

NO CHARGE

My blasted battery's run out
I checked it yesterday,
It's not like lots of people call
To hear what I might say.
I hardly ever use it
There's no need to wonder why,
It's totally frustrating
And I think I'm going to cry.
"You must have a Smart Phone"
That's what my friends all said
So I went out and bought one
Must be softening in the head.
I cannot even work it
As when I switch it on
It baffles me with questions
I think it's a total con.
And even when I turn it off
It doesn't cut the power
But it spends the whole time talking
To the nearest cell phone tower.
Then when I want to use it
It hasn't any juice
So I would like to ask you
Is a Smart Phone any use?

MISSION IMPOSSIBLE

There's cheese inside this wrapper,
But I can't get it out,
I've got the crackers ready
And I'll enjoy them, I've no doubt.
I've tried to snip the corner,
But not an inch will give
I've struggled now for half an hour
And I've lost the will to live.

There's milk inside this carton,
But I can't get it out,
My cereal is waiting
But I can't form the spout.
I've used a pair of scissors,
Totally in vain
And now I've dropped it in the sink
And it's all gone down the drain.

There's bacon in this packet,
But I can't get it out,
I wanted a 'Full English'
Now, I just can't mess about.
I grabbed a nice, sharp, carving knife,
Well, it's always worked before
But suddenly it slipped, and now –
I'm bleeding on the floor.

There are pills in this container
But I can't get them out,
I take them 'cos they keep me calm
And curb my urge to SHOUT.
These tops I'm told are 'childproof',
But of everyone alive
The only ones who open them
Are children under five.

There's champagne in this bottle
But I can't get it out,
I'm getting rather desperate now –
My tongue is hanging out.
I've tried to use the corkscrew,
And now that's stuck as well
I'll have to try another one
Dammit all to hell!

There's a man in a laboratory
But I can't get him out,
He developed all this packaging
To keep bacteria out.
The problem that he overlooked,
(Which wasn't his intention)
Is nobody has found a way
To open his invention.

IT'S ALL REPEATS AT CHRISTMAS

(Sung to 'The Twelve Days of Christmas')

On the first day of Christmas, I served up for our tea
A free-range turkey feeding forty-three.

On the second day of Christmas, I served up for our tea
Fifty turkey sarnies from a free-range turkey feeding forty-three.

On the third day of Christmas, I served up for our tea
Sixty turkey burgers, fifty turkey sarnies, from a free-range turkey feeding forty-three.

On the fourth day of Christmas, I served up for our tea
Eighty turkey fritters, sixty turkey burgers, fifty turkey sarnies from a free-range turkey feeding forty-three.

On the fifth day of Christmas, I served up for our tea
Ten pints of soup.
Eighty turkey fritters, sixty turkey burgers, fifty turkey sarnies, from a free-range turkey feeding forty-three.

On the sixth day of Christmas, I served up for our tea
My stupid partner, who had bought the turkey feeding forty-three.

There's only two of us.......
Well, one now..........
The other one's gone.
Finished..........
I wish that blasted turkey was.

ANYONE FOR TENA'S?™

An elderly friend said to me
"I wish I was still twenty-three.
And while you may scoff,
I'm frightened to cough –
As each time I do it, I pee".

A lady whose name was Louise
Told me "Getting old isn't a breeze,
When years pass as seconds,
Incontinence beckons
So I've trained myself never to sneeze."

An Australian friend's up the creek
As her urinary system is weak
When she hears something funny
She runs for the dunny
Laughing causes her bladder to leak.

WHAT'S THAT?

Why do pubs and restaurants serve food that's so
pretentious?
I find that it makes eating out appallingly contentious.
After I've perused the menu, I don't fancy much of that
Which, if I'm with my husband, always ends up in a spat.
I'll do my best to pick a dish, and I do try to decide
But why are pubs so keen to serve up food that's
poncified?
They will offer 'Seafood Medley with Chef's Sauce', to
keep you guessing
But isn't that just crab and prawns with Thousand Island
Dressing?
There's 'Chicken Liver Parfait' or 'Confit of Free-Range
Duck',
Or 'Crispy Chilli Calamari', of which they've run out, with
luck.
Try 'Cauliflower au Gratin' with tomatoes, chips and peas
But I remember when we called it 'Cauliflower Cheese'

And what could be the reason I would sample 'Tapenade'?
I've checked out the ingredients, saying "No" would not be
hard.
But it isn't just the Starters, it's the Main Courses as well
I'm really not adventurous, as no doubt you can tell
As I like simple food that's easily identified
And not a piece of Cod that's been completely poncified.

Now nobody makes gravy like my mother used to do
Instead everything I order has a different type of 'Jus',
I don't think there's any difference, as I think they have a plan
To add an extra fiver on as often as they can.
What happened to Ham, Egg and Chips, Steak Pies and Casseroles?
Now it's Pasta and Risotto that are always served in bowls,
The pasta's done 'al dente', if you don't know what that means
It's 'very slightly undercooked' (!) in many haute cuisines.
There's meat I've never heard of, unknown fish that they will fry

And smother them with sauces that completely poncify.
Now, don't think requesting salad's going to get you off the hook
They've the oddest of ingredients, if you dare to take a look,
Arugula, shaved fennel and dandelion leaves
I wouldn't want to meet the chef in whose brain that conceives.
The salad comes with dressing which they don't serve in a pot
So they've poured it over everything, if you want it or not.
I think my safe solution is to always eat at home
As I don't think pubs and restaurants are where I want to roam
So, I guess the best that I can do is go on walking by
Establishments with menus that they need to poncify.

CLASS ACT

M'sister, Pyracantha, has a fondness for brown ale
She karate chops the bottle tops, but never breaks a nail,
As she gets it down her neck in less than thirty seconds flat
There's never time to ask her "Do you want a glass with
that?"

Her favourite she gets by the crate and keeps it by the
bed,
She has often been the worse for wear, although I haven't
said,
I find it near impossible but feel I have to try
And prevent her lobbing empties at the people passing by.

I hoped that she would try champagne and get a little posh
But she rejected my suggestion saying bubbles cost more dosh,
And despite my better efforts and a very cunning plan
She now drinks cider, extra strong, directly from the can.

(Author's note: This comic verse is not about my actual sister, but a virtual sister.

She told me to say that.

Virtually.)

BARKING MAD

I'm not a hypochondriac, it's just I'm always ill,
I wake up every morning thinking "Well, I'm breathing still".
If it's a Saturday, it's neck pain, on a Wednesday arm or back
I have a chart of ailments, to ensure that I keep track.
I always have a flu jab, I get mine with Clubcard points,
And while I'm in the chemists I'll buy something for my joints.
Glucosamine's the answer, I take vitamins as well
If I wasn't always poorly, I'd be healthy, you can tell.
I'm on first names with the Doctor, he really knows all my complaints
From athlete's foot and earache, to my funny little faints.
He's always had the time for me, when dishing out my pills
And lotions, creams and ointments, which ease my pains and chills.
I get tissues for my nosebleeds which happen every day,
But now the Doctor's been suggesting that I should stay away.
He's removed me from his list so a new practice I must find
I was thinking I'd change anyway, their receptionist's unkind.
She says I "imagine illness, and my health is an obsession"
Perhaps I'll smack her round the face, to teach her some discretion.
They've appeared to put the word out, no one else will take me on
So any loyalty I felt is well and truly gone.
I'm going to the vet now, Doctor's passed on all my notes
But his treatment is expensive, so I'm asking him for quotes.
He thinks I've got distemper, and a dose of kennel cough
Though he tells me not to worry, I may well be finished off.

It would really be ironic if the thing that popped my clogs
Was a medical professional used to treating cats and dogs.

FUNNY YOU SHOULD ASK........PART 2

Are topless women reading newspapers, keeping abreast of The Times?

Would you say that bras are booby-traps?

Is telling a man he has no hair, speaking the bald truth?

Are obviously wealthy people, who always travel by cab, prepared to pay hire taxis?

To gardeners, are moles a pain in the grass?

Do brunettes and redheads find life isn't fair?

Is Pinocchio a wooden actor?

On Valentine's Day, if you are given a Victoria sponge, a tub of custard and a pot of cream, is someone trifling with your affections?

When a pencil draws a conclusion, does it have a point?

If a play on words burps loudly, should you pardon the pun?

GREAT EXPECTATIONS

My grandson Joe, asked me today
"Grandma, are you going away?
'Cos Dad told me you're leaving soon
He's hoping you'll be gone by June.

Now, as you say you love me so,
I think there's something you should know
I want some money in your will
Come on Grandma, take your pill."

My Mum and Dad don't have much cash
And they can't help me to look flash,
So I thought I'd wheedle good old Gran
Who really is my biggest fan.

"There's lots of things I want to buy
As I should be a 'trendy guy',
Designer labels, iPhone X –
The one with all the latest specs.

You want me happy, looking smart
So, when do you think you'll depart?
I'll miss you when you're up in Heaven".
Joe's lucky if he reaches seven.

('orrible little sod!)

BITE ME

I didn't think I'd ever wish for dentures
As they always seemed to me the last resort,
But resulting from my dentist's latest ventures
I'm going to need them sooner than I thought.

I've always been most careful with my brushing
And I floss for hours 'til plaque's no longer there,
So the speed of tooth loss now is really crushing
And suddenly my mouth looks rather bare.

I've still got teeth that I can use for smiling
Which I flash when any friends come into view,
But even though I may look quite beguiling
I'm running out of those I need to chew.

So, no more crunchy carrots, pears, or apples
Crackling never more will pass my lips,
I'm in terror, at the dentist, while he grapples
With my remaining teeth, in pliers, which he grips.

But my pleasure with my false teeth has been fleeting
Though I'm sure that I'll accept them, in due course
While I imagined they'd assist me with my eating –
They've got me starring in the Panto, as the Horse.

DON'T RUSH ME

My husband says he doesn't faff – that's patently untrue
He'll take five hours to start a job that I'd have done in two.
There is a tool for every job, which isn't euphemistic
But hoping he'll know where they are, proves wildly optimistic.
He has more bits of wood than anyone I've ever met,
But the right piece for the job's not been identified, as yet.
The task he's doing "Won't take long" and he's absolutely right
But the time spent looking for his drill goes on into the night.
And still, when morning comes, he hasn't found the blasted thing
It must be me who's moved it, and my neck he'd like to wring.
And when, at last, it comes to light, a sheepish look he'll give
So it isn't any wonder that I lose the will to live.
He'll never get A into G before it's half past four,
Then he thunders like an elephant around the bedroom floor
Until I get most anxious, with a very sinking feeling
That it won't be long before I see him crashing through the ceiling.
Although these "projects" take him months, he does a splendid job
So I almost wish I didn't want to smack him in the gob.

'APPLE'™ SAUCE

I'm sending you this message from my iPad
It's a gadget that I bought the other day
It does everything a person could ask of it
And fulfils it in the most efficient way.

It will tell you if I'm sending you an email
It will tell me if you're sending me a text
It's such a clever item of equipment
That it even tells me what I'm doing next.

I can use it when I want to check my banking
Which I have to say I do find rather funny
But it sometimes rather oversteps the boundaries
When it attempts to tell me how to spend my money.

It's very handy when I'm on vacation
I play games and things if ever I get bored
And it leaves more room for shoes inside my suitcase
If I don't want to take a thousand books abroad.

But, the downside is it's very anti-social
As I can take it every single place I go
So I shan't be having any conversations
Unless it's on my iPad, don't you know.

And to ensure you are aware that I have got one
I will tell you in a way that's very clear
On every single message that I write you
"I've sent this from my iPad", will appear.

VEGETABLE MEDLEY

There was a young man from Devizes
Whose onions were various sizes
But to his dismay
When put on display
His marrow won all of the prizes.

CINDERELLA

When I was two, I liked a shoe
That featured funny faces,
When I was six and full of tricks
Knew how to tie my laces.
Into my teens without the means
To fund my love of sandals,
Bought espadrilles - they're flat, no thrills
My feet thought they were vandals.
When I hit twenty boots were plenty
Worn with skirts mid-thigh,
If boys were near - this you would hear:
A loud collective sigh.
Reaching thirty, bought shoes flirty
With vertiginous high heels,
From five foot ten looked down on men
Imagine how that feels!
Pushing forty, somewhat naughty
Spent a vast amount,
Red lacquered soles left gaping holes
Inside my bank account.
When I was fifty and still nifty
Really knew my onions,
I had nice feet, dainty and neat
Not compromised by bunions.
At fifty-eight, there's no debate
Stilettos were my passion,
I'm rather tall - it's far to fall
Should comfort conquer fashion?
Leaving sixty, feet still pixie
Corns are yet to beckon,
Books I peruse for Jimmy Choo's
A last chance, do you reckon?
Reaching eighty somewhat weighty

Bending over's in the past,
I must tell you, flat, slip-on shoe
Makes stylish sense, at last.

TRIVIAL PURSUIT

*(The Entire Story In the Most Tedious Detail You Can Possibly Imagine.
But I Know You're Interested)*

I have a page on Facebook that I update every night
As I'm certain people want to read every word I write.
I blog about my wardrobe and what I plan to wear
I know that you are interested in how I've styled my hair.
If I go out in the evening and I'm feeling in the pink
I'll tell you where I'm going, and how much I have to drink
The contents of my breakfast, and lunch and dinner too
Are just the sort of details that I'll pass on to you.
I'm always on my iPad, it goes everywhere with me
So I can keep you up to date with triviality.
You all should be so grateful for minutiae I share
For if you're being honest, you just wish that you were there.
Now I'm out for coffee and I'm watching from my seat
So I can write and tell you all what other people eat.
The ladies in the corner have another round of cake
And the fellow at the counter really should have stomach ache.
He's had three cups of coffee which he slowly drinks in sips
And extra crispy bacon with a triple egg and chips.
He's ordering a pudding, (so I'm telling cyberspace)
With a second jug of custard, that he's shoving in his face.
I think it's quite disgusting he can sit and eat all that
So I'm blogging to my followers "No wonder he is fat".
Oh, I think he's coming over, so I'd better close the screen
If he sees what I've been typing, he may well cause a scene.
A question now to ask you and I promise I'm not bitter
Why do they call it 'Tweeting' when the platform is called 'Twitter'?
If I am not mistaken, and this tickles me a bit
You can't be called a 'Tweeter' you are just a silly 'Twit'.

There's nothing that's too tedious, for me to share with you,
So why don't you reciprocate and bore me senseless too?
We'll all meet up on Facebook, please, ensure we keep it civil
Then you and I can chat as 'friends' and swap our mindless drivel.

TAKING THE MOCHA

I went into a café yesterday,
But the place I chose just filled me with dismay,
I only wanted basic coffee
Not with hazelnuts or toffee,
But all the choices put my brain in disarray.
There's Caffé Caramella,
Or Hot Chocolate with Marshmella (sorry!)
And Americano, Latte or Flat White,
Double Chocolate Cookie Mocha
Full of caffeine - what a shocker!
And it's guaranteed I'll stay awake all night.
Do I want Medium, Large or Small?
Oh, what the heck, I'll take them all
In china mugs or cardboard cups to go?
I think I've lost my voice
As I'm bewildered by the choice,
And if I was young, a tantrum I would throw.
The barista said to me
"Would you prefer a cup of tea?"
And I have to say, that sounded just like heaven
But then she spoilt it all
When she said "If I recall
The choices there are limited to seven.
I've got Earl or Lady Grey
Gunpowder tea" - I'm blown away!
And I'm thinking, how can I get out of here?
"Lapsang or Jasmine, very scented"
Now I'm feeling quite demented
Do I drink the stuff? Or dab behind my ear?
"There's Peppermint to help digestion......"
I almost made a rude suggestion
If I smack her, could I claim it's self-defence?
As I was walking out the door

She shouted "Wait, there's just one more
We've Chamomile, if you are feeling tense".
I teetered on the brink
I only want a simple drink,
And I really don't have any more to give,
There isn't any time
As today, I've passed my prime
And thanks to her, I've lost the will to live.

WASN'T ME

My husband has a secret friend
He keeps away from me,
But whenever anything goes wrong
It's always "Somebody".
"Somebody" left the gas on
And forgot to lock the door,
He left the windows open
So the rain had soaked the floor.
"Somebody's" moved his wallet
Had his car keys, and his phone,
But it's strange it only happens
When "Somebody's" alone.
"Somebody's" got his glasses
And the key that locks the shed,
After hours of fruitless searching
"Somebody'd" put them 'neath the bed.
My husband never takes the blame
He always says "It's you",
But why would I hide three hammers
And seven tubes of glue?
"Somebody" drops stuff on the floor
Doesn't notice where it lands,
I often wonder if
He'd find his bottom, with both hands.
Perhaps he'll introduce me
To this man, who plagues him so,
But I will wager when we meet
It's "Somebody" I know.

MILES AWAY

When I was young, my grandma said, "It's no fun getting
old"
But as that seemed light years away, the idea didn't hold.
I could walk unaided so I didn't need a cane
And had the vaguest notion what constituted pain.
But, I am getting old now, and it's quite true what she said,
And I encounter problems when I'm getting out of bed.
I cannot get my slippers on, the floor's too far away
I'm sure that it was closer even up till yesterday.
There comes a time I think that there is very little point
To overstretch and aggravate another nagging joint.
Now bending over isn't very easy any more
And if I am unfortunate, drop something on the floor
I'll count to ten and wait, then I will say a little prayer
To try and think of something else to do, while I'm down
there.

T(APPING)

Diana had a Smart Phone, as did her brother John
And all their friends and families, and always kept them on
They took them on the buses and they took them on the
train
Their Smart Phones told them everything, like is it going to
rain?
The youngsters of today take all these gadgets in their
stride
But I can't fathom how they work, and heaven knows, I've
tried
Each time I turn my Smart Phone on, it just tells me to wait
So I go and ask my neighbour's son, a clever boy, who's
eight.
Now I was at a funeral, just the other day
A place where you'd expect that folks would put their
phones away
We're just about to say goodbye amidst the candle flickers
A Smart Phone beeped, and yes, you've guessed, it was
the ruddy vicar's.
Diana and her 'bestest' friend, a lady known as Jenny
Were going off on holiday, so saving every penny
The Smart Phone helped them budget and maintain their
bank accounts
By only letting them take cash in very small amounts.
John and his friends like clubbing and hanging round in
bars
The Smart Phone helps them choose their drinks and pays
to park their cars
If the music is so deafening that all the friends get vexed
The Smart Phone has the answer, it sends everyone a
text.
The Smart Phone will do anything if you download the
'app'
Update you on 'celebrities' and other useless crap.

It will give you scrummy recipes, do shopping, best of all
To save you getting out of bed, turns lights off, in the hall.
It will tell you what the weather's like in London and Hong Kong
And when your partner's late from work, and whether he'll be long
You can check up with your mum, did she forget to feed the cat?
And half a million other very useful things like that.
You can ask it for directions as you walk along the street
There's an 'app' to tell you how to cope with bunions on your feet
And if you are unlucky and have any parts that swell
No doubt there'll be an 'app' to help you manage that as well.
If you want to check your horoscope or see a piece of art
Perhaps you need advice on how to mend a broken heart
And should you require reminding of the place you left your cap
You've got a Smart Phone, all you have to do is 'tap the app'.
People's lives are on their Smart Phones, each appointment and each date
And all the times are programmed in so that they're never late.
If dining out, the phone will check they don't eat too much starch
So be afraid, be much afraid, Smart Phones are on the march.
It will start the central heating and put on the clothes to wash
And take a load of messages in voices that are posh,
But I really have to wonder, and I'm sure I'm not alone
Does anyone remember that it's actually a phone?

IS IT ME?

Any other Colours?

A pointless question, on which I'll risk a fiver,
Please tell me if the same occurs to you:
To be a Navy Seal or Navy Diver
Do you have to be a certain shade of blue?

Conundrum

Here's a little query – I've always wondered why
'Buffalo Wings' are so called, when buffalos can't fly?
Another thing that's doubtful, although in my brain it lingers
I haven't seen a fish with hands, never mind with fingers.

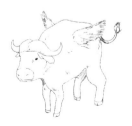 

Try It

Why do people say "Reversing back"?
When there isn't any other way to go
If anybody out there has the knack
Of reversing forward, I would like to know.

Sticky End

To be a plastic surgeon's no mean feat
Tweaking noses, boobs and botties 'til they're neat,
But have you ever felt
Plastic surgeons ought to melt
If you leave them unattended in the heat?

Cheerio!

I had breakfast today with the Millers
Who are writers of popular thrillers,
As we ate our cornflakes
I was asked if that makes
Us a trio of cereal killers?

SORRY, I DIDN'T CATCH THAT.......

My husband never listens to a single word I say
He sits there looking vacant, then goes off on his way,
But something happened recently that caused an awful fuss
As despite my frantic warnings, he was knocked down by a bus.
I told the inquest later that it wasn't all my fault
For I'd called out, very urgently, and loudly, he must halt.
His reaction was quite simply what he always used to do
Which was carry on, regardless, as the bus drove into view.
I saw the look of horror on the driver's startled face
As my husband flew up in the air and onwards into space.
The driver said I pushed him, which was totally untrue
As that is something wicked, which I'd never, ever do.
I hope that where he landed is a place where folks don't talk
But I bet he wished he'd listened, on his final, fatal walk.

COLOUR BLAND

I bought a pair of trainers, so they'd help my feet go places
A boring shade of black, but tied with lovely neon laces,
My husband took one look and said "Since you're now sixty-eight
Don't you think that you should purchase items rather more sedate?"

I've always loved bright colours – scarlet, blue and green and pink
And I don't really care at all what other people think,
But there are several tones I've always viewed with total scorn
That's beige and taupe and natural, as they masquerade as 'fawn'.

I know I'm getting on a bit, horizons now more narrow
But I'm still a Bird of Paradise, not drab and dreary sparrow,
So keep your unkind comments, let them stay inside your head
And you can dress me in your 'neutrals', after I am dead.

GRAVITY

My boobs are heading for my feet
They're racing down there, as I speak
Both closely followed by my tum
But slightly beaten by my bum.

I used to be described as "pert"
With boobs quite upright, on alert
But that was in the distant past
And everything's now sagging, fast.

Perhaps the answer's in a corset,
And all my flesh inside I'll force it
If far too tight, I'm sure I'll burst
So, everyone – expect the worst.

I'd go off bang, just fancy that
And all around are showered with fat
When all that's left is empty skin
Remember me, when I was thin.

LOITERING WITH INTENT

(This was written during the first Covid lockdown in 2020, just in case we've forgotten what shopping was like during that time!!!)

I'm really not in the mood to queue
As I've certainly got better things I could do
Outside Tesco we're inching our way to the door
Now it's twenty past six, and I've been here since four.

I'm really not in the mood to queue
But we've run out of loo rolls, so there is a clue
We're being quite careful what everyone eats
As my husband's decided to ration the sheets.

I'm really not in the mood to queue
Hugo's emptied the wine rack, quite "out of the blue"
He's gone through the vodka, the gin and the beer
Can anyone tell me what I'm doing here?

I'm really not in the mood to queue
Now I've only just noticed a hole in my shoe
My foot's getting wet, oh, this waiting's a pain
And to make matters worse, now it's pelting with rain.

I'm really not in the mood to queue
Thought I'd finished the list, just remembered shampoo
There's a line for the checkout, stop sinking my heart
I see fifteen in front, at two metres apart.

I'm really not in the mood to queue
As it's desperately boring, what's your point of view?
While I'm patiently waiting, this gives me a blast -
The clanking of bottles as trolleys go past.

I'm really not in the mood to queue
But if I have to do it, the same goes for you
Don't try pushing in front or I'll give you a smack
And I'll show you your place - which is right at the back.

BOGOFF

We're back in lockdown from today
And I think it's fairly safe to say
That supermarkets need patrols
To stop bulk buys of toilet rolls.

There's plenty there for all of us
But selfish people cause the fuss,
And turn the population manic
By buying Andrex in a panic.

And where do these folks store them all
In bathroom, cloakroom, lounge and hall?
Why do they need to buy in tonnes?
It's Coronavirus – not 'the runs'.

What I would like the shops to do
And I think this might appeal to you,
Is catch these people in the act
And shame them, without any tact.

"Attention shoppers" they should say
Through the tannoy they use every day,
"There's a panic buyer, checkout two"
So the rest of us could hiss and boo.

A social conscience they all lack
And should be made to put them back,
So when we do what we must do
We'll know there's paper by the loo.

AND YOU ARE........?

Teresa Green and Robin Banks
Won't give their parents many thanks.
But Hazel Nutt and Willy Nili?
Unfortunate, or just plain silly?
Primrose Hill and Justin Case
Will go through life quite red of face.
While Edna Bagg and Andy Mann
Should change their names soon as they can.
Poor Olive Branch and Cherry Tartt
If that was you, where would you start?
A family jewel is Precious Stone
Well, rather that than Nora Bone.
I really pity Polly Ester:
Can't you feel resentment fester?
I'm hoping that you're keeping track
Or you can go to Helen Back.
There's one more name for me to mock
But I don't envy Dana Sock.

FLYING FISH

(This is a true story)

"As summer's here", my husband said, "I'll tell you what we'll do,
I've decided that we need to buy a new gas barbecue.
I'm tired of using charcoal as it takes too long to heat,
By the time the food is ready, I've got no desire to eat".
So, we go to find a new one, and spend some hours looking
Then suddenly he said to me "I'm going to do the cooking.
I've made a joint decision that this will be MY toy".
I looked on in amazement, and then I jumped for joy!
The first time that he used it, we invited friends around
When they saw my husband cooking, nobody made a sound.
I'd bought some steak and chicken, put a fish inside a kettle
My husband put it on to cook, including all the metal.
He turned the burners up to full, then closed the barbie lid
And sat there chatting cheerfully, I promise you he did.
I'm not supposed to interrupt, but thought I'd risk his ire
As I felt he'd want to know the food appeared to be on fire.
He opened up the top and then he lifted out the fish,
Then with a yell, his wrist he gave an unexpected swish.
As he's not used to cooking, here's a thing he hadn't planned
You put metal handles over flames, you're going to burn your hand.
The trout sailed across the garden, I thought "he's being overzealous"
And it ended up in pieces, ricocheting off the trellis.
He tried to brush the dirt off, put the remnants on a plate
But I told him in the strongest words that it was far too late.
Due to this distraction, he'd forgotten all the meat
And in his haste to save the fish, had not turned down the heat.

The steaks were tiny charcoal lumps, the chicken past decline,
So we had bread and salad. And an awful lot of wine.
The next time that we asked our friends, I told them I would cook
I think that they were quite relieved, as they exchanged a look.
And though, in truth, I have to claim I'm an efficient lass
He hadn't checked the cylinder, and we ran out of gas.

SIGNS OF THE TIMES

When I stood on the bathroom scales, I couldn't help but
moan
For they were telling me that I had put on several stone
I'm sure I'm still the slender girl I was at twenty-three
So I'm convinced the bathroom scales are telling lies to
me.

When I looked in the mirror, I could not hold back a groan
For staring right back at me was a grey haired, wrinkled
crone
I thought I'd see the blue eyed blonde I was at thirty-three
So I'm convinced the bathroom mirror's telling lies to me.

FUNNY YOU SHOULD ASK.........PART 3

Do shoplifters pause and take stock?

An example of a rhetorical question: How are you?

Is the final page in a travel brochure, the last resort?

If you have grave concerns, is cremation the answer?

Is rigor mortice a stiff lock?

Who are the faeries away with?

If I charge friends for my homemade conserve, am I a jam tart?

If Sam and Ella invite you to supper, would you say you were sick?

NATURALLY

Because I am a natural blonde
Folk think my IQ's lowly
So when they start to speak to me
They do it very slowly.
They'll never use two syllables
As most think one will do
And male shop assistants
Are guilty of it too.
An example here to show you
I was looking for a phone
And a callow youth came up to me
Annoyed me with his tone.
I told him what I wanted
And he went away to think
Then he told me "I've got just the phone
And best of all, it's pink.
I assume your hair is natural
And not colour from a bottle?"
I wonder why I get the urge
Patronising men to throttle.
He said "These are the instructions
You will find them complicating"
I replied "I'm not a bimbo
If that's what you're insinuating"
I'd not let him upset me
But took hours of his time
Then went and bought it somewhere else –
Revenge was quite sublime.

ABOUT THE AUTHOR…..

(see following pages)

ABOUT THE AUTHOR

1 - MY LIFE AND CAREERS

I was born at a very young age. This happy event was a total shock to my mother as she had no idea she was pregnant and thought it was just the way her coat was fastened.

I have written Comic Verse and nonsense jottings for a very long time. I live in a yurt just outside Bath, have been married several times, and just buried my fifth husband.

In a shallow grave in Epping Forest.

He will be sadly missed.

Until I line up number six.

I have had an interesting life, a highlight of which was when I appeared as a fire-eating unicyclist in the circus. I thrilled the crowds with my act, but sadly, on one occasion, had a sneezing fit at an inopportune moment. This resulted in the Big Top burning to the ground, and me being asked to leave. I later got a job in a firework factory, but that didn't work out either because I blew it up after mistaking the gunpowder for coffee.

I worked briefly as a Tour Guide, which came to an abrupt halt when I realised I had misunderstood the term 'Escort'.

For a while, I was employed in a fast-food restaurant, but was sacked for being slow. I then applied for the position of short-order cook.

I was unsuccessful.

Apparently, I'm too tall.

That was followed by a few performances as a ventriloquist, which regrettably never really took off as people couldn't tell which one of us was the dummy.

I'm thinking of retiring now as no one seems to want a 90-year-old lounge singer, who can lounge, but can't sing.

(Some or all of the above may not be true, but no husbands have been deliberately harmed in any way or by any means – Your Honour)!

continued….

ABOUT THE AUTHOR

2 - MY CHILDREN

My children have had many varied careers, and until I visited my oldest son Geronimo, in Parkhurst, I thought 'Her Majesty's Pleasure' was a nightclub, as several of his siblings spent much time there.

Geronimo has an identical twin sister, Pocahontas, although they are never seen together, as she is his alter ego. Their brother, Aladdin, sleeps upright in the cupboard under the stairs. Unfortunately, he does have a rather disconcerting habit of jumping out at people shouting: "He's behind you". His psychiatrist has said that he will grow out of it, but seeing he is now 52, his father, Widow Twankey, and I, have our doubts.

My favourite child, although I admit I shouldn't have one, is Quasimodo, who has a very lucrative career as a private detective. He has recently gone into partnership with his brother Pinocchio, and they make a winning combination as Quasimodo always goes with a hunch, and Pinocchio can smell a rat from miles away.

Then there is Houdini, known in the family as "Whodunnit", as he was always in trouble. He spent his entire youth escaping from the house by various means, never realising that all he had to do was open the front door and walk out. Bright he isn't. He is currently emulating his namesake by going over Niagara Falls in a barrel. Regrettably, he didn't realise it was attached to a bungee cord, and for the last three weeks has been going up and down at a worrying speed. The last time I heard from him, he was feeling extremely dizzy and had been sick all down his Winnie the Pooh pyjamas.

My least favourite daughter is Cyanide, as she has an acid tongue and can't be tolerated even in small doses. Ultimately, time spent with her is a painful experience.

As seven of her husbands have found out.

The quads are Felonious, Erroneous, Oblivious and Dick. Felonious has a habit of 'borrowing' other people's things, Erroneous usually gets hold of the wrong end of the stick, Oblivious hasn't a clue, and the least said about Dick, the better. Their father, Juan Cornetto, is a well-known local businessman I met while on a brief holiday in Venice. I wouldn't say the earth moved, but water definitely slopped over the side of the gondola.

If I'm honest, I have so many offspring, I forget who most of them are until the police turn up checking alibis. Their fathers include: a High Court Judge, several Members of Parliament, the local football team and the men who empty the bins, but, in my defence, there's not much to do here on Wednesdays.

Or any other day, come to that.

The End

(If you enjoyed reading this collection of comic verse, please leave me a review and/or let me know by email at:

dbw2022@btinternet.com).

Printed in Great Britain
by Amazon

24755395R00050